Brittany johnson

A

Walt Disney's
Donald Duck
at the Toy Store

Written by Joan Phillips

Illustrated by Willy Ito, Claudia Mielnik, and Roy Wilson

A Golden Book • New York
Western Publishing Company, Inc., Racine, Wisconsin 53404

Huey, Dewey, and Louie
were not happy.
"Why are you so sad?"
asked Donald.
"We have nothing to do,"
said Huey.

"Why don't you play?"
asked Donald.
"Why don't you play
with your toys?"
"We are tired of
the same old toys,"
said Dewey.
"Very, very tired," said Louie.

"We will go
to the toy store,"
said Donald.
"We will get
some new toys."
"Hurray!"
said Huey, Dewey,
and Louie.

"Here is a good toy.
Can we get this?"
asked Huey.

"I will try it
for you,"
said Donald.

"No, Uncle Donald!
Stop! Stop!
Do not jump.
Do not jump
in the store.
Watch out, Uncle Donald!"

"That toy is not good,"
said Donald.
"That toy is not good
for you."

"Here is a good toy,"
said Dewey.
"Can we get these skates?"

"I will try them,"
said Donald.

"No, Uncle Donald!
Stop! Stop!
Do not skate.
Do not skate
in the store.
Watch out, Uncle Donald!"

"Those skates are not good,"
said Donald.
"Those skates are not good
for you."

"Here is a good toy,"
said Louie.
"Can we get this
big, big balloon?"

"I will try it,"
said Donald.

"No, Uncle Donald!
Stop! Stop!
You must not play.
You must not play
in the store.
Watch out, Uncle Donald!"

"So many toys!"
said Donald.
"I will try this bike.
I will try these paints.
I will try lots of toys!"

"Stop, Mr. Duck!
Stop! Stop!"

"Not now,"
said Donald.
"I must try this car!
I must try this kite!"

"Your uncle must go,"
said the storekeeper.
"Can you make him
go now?"

"Uncle Donald,
we must go home,"
said Huey, Dewey, and Louie.
"We must go home now."
"Not now,"
said Donald.
"I must try this train!"

"Please, please!
Make him go!"
said the storekeeper.
"I will give you these toys
if you make him go."
"Hurray!"
said Huey, Dewey, and Louie.

"Look, Uncle Donald.
Look at our new toys!
You can play with these toys
at home!"
"No," said Donald.
"I am tired of toys.
Very, very tired."